CHILDREN'S THRIFT CLASSICS

Chinese Fairy Tales

FREDERICK H. MARTENS

Illustrated by Yuko Green

DOVER PUBLICATIONS, INC.
Mineola, New York

DOVER CHILDREN'S THRIFT CLASSICS
GENERAL EDITOR: PAUL NEGRI

Bibliographical Note

Chinese Fairy Tales is a new selection of stories adapted from *The Chinese Fairy Book,* Frederick A. Stokes Company, New York, 1921. The illustrations and note have been prepared specially for this edition.

Library of Congress Cataloging-in-Publication Data

Martens, Frederick Herman, 1874–1932.
   Chinese fairy tales / Frederick H. Martens.
      p.   cm. — (Dover children's thrift classics)
   Contents: Women's words part flesh and blood — The three rhymsters — The bird with nine heads — The cave of the beasts — The panther — The great flood — Why dog and cat are enemies — The herd boy and the weaving maiden — The lady of the moon — The miserly farmer — Old Dschang — The flower-elves — The dragon-princess — The disowned princess — The maiden who was stolen away — The frog princess.
   Summary: Tales selected and adapted from The Chinese fairy book, published in 1921.
   ISBN 0-486-40140-5 (pbk.)
   1. Tales—China. [1. Folklore—China.] I. Title. II. Series.
PZ8.1.M367Ch 1998
398.2'0951—dc21
                                                       97–42626
                                                             CIP
                                                             AC

Manufactured in the United States of America
Dover Publications, Inc., 31 East 2nd Street, Mineola, N.Y. 11501

Contents

An enormous Roc came rushing down,
took the ear in his beak and flew away.

Women's Words Part Flesh and Blood

O NCE UPON A TIME there were two brothers, who lived in the same house. And the big brother listened to his wife's words, and because of them fell out with the little one. Summer had begun, and the time for sowing the high-growing millet had come. The little brother had no grain, and asked the big one to loan him some, and the big one ordered his wife to give it to him. But she took the grain, put it in a large pot and cooked it until it was done. Then she gave it to the little fellow. He knew nothing about it, and went and sowed his field with it. Yet, since the grain had been cooked, it did not sprout. Only a single grain of seed had not been cooked; so only a single sprout shot up. The little brother was hard-working and industrious by nature, and hence he watered and hoed the sprout all day long. And the sprout grew mightily, like a tree, and an ear of millet sprang up out of it like a canopy, large enough to shade half an acre of ground. In the fall the ear was ripe. Then the little brother took his ax and chopped it down. But no sooner had the ear fallen to the ground, than an enormous Roc came rushing down, took the ear in his beak and flew away. The little brother ran after him as far as the shore of the sea.

Then the bird turned and spoke to him like a human being, as follows: "You should not seek to harm me! What is this one ear worth to you? East of the sea is the isle of gold and silver. I will carry you across. There you may take whatever you want, and become very rich."

The little brother was satisfied, and climbed on the bird's back, and the latter told him to close his eyes. So he only heard the air whistling past his ears, as though he were driving through a strong wind, and beneath him the roar and surge of flood and waves. Suddenly the bird settled on a rock: "Here we are!" he said.

Then the little brother opened his eyes and looked about him: and on all sides he saw nothing but the radiance and shimmer of all sorts of white and yellow objects. He took about a dozen of the little things and hid them in his breast.

"Have you enough?" asked the Roc.

"Yes, I have enough," he replied.

"That is well," answered the bird. "Moderation protects one from harm."

Then he once more took him up, and carried him back again.

When the little brother reached home, he bought himself a good piece of ground in the course of time, and became quite well-to-do.

But his brother was jealous of him, and said to him, harshly: "Where did you manage to steal the money?"

So the little one told him the whole truth of the matter. Then the big brother went home and took counsel with his wife.

"Nothing easier," said his wife. "I will just cook grain again and keep back one seedling so that it is not done. Then you shall sow it, and we will see what happens."

No sooner said than done. And sure enough, a single sprout shot up, and sure enough, the sprout bore a single ear of millet, and when harvest time came around, the Roc again appeared and carried it off in his beak. The big brother was pleased, and ran after him, and the

There the big brother saw the gold and silver heaped up everywhere.

Roc said the same thing he had said before, and carried the big brother to the island. There the big brother saw the gold and silver heaped up everywhere. The largest pieces were like hills, the small ones were like bricks, and the real tiny ones were like grains of sand. They blinded his eyes. He only regretted that he knew of no way by which he could move mountains. So he bent down and picked up as many pieces as possible.

The Roc said: "Now you have enough! You will over-tax your strength."

"Have patience but a little while longer," said the big brother. "Do not be in such a hurry! I must get a few more pieces!"

And thus time passed.

The Roc again urged him to make haste: "The sun will appear in a moment," said he, "and the sun is so hot it burns human beings up."

"Wait just a little while longer," said the big brother. But that very moment a red disk broke through the clouds with tremendous power. The Roc flew into the sea, stretched out both his wings, and beat the water with them in order to escape the heat. But the big brother was shrivelled up by the sun.

Note: The Roc is called *pong* in Chinese, and the treasures on the island are spoken of as "all sorts of yellow and white objects" because the little brother does not know that they are gold and silver.

The Three Rhymsters

O NCE THERE WERE three daughters in a family. The oldest one married a physician, the second one married a magistrate; but the third, who was more than usually intelligent and a clever talker, married a farmer.

Now it chanced, once upon a time, that their parents were celebrating a birthday. So the three daughters came, together with their husbands, to wish them long life and happiness. The parents-in-law prepared a meal for their three sons-in-law, and put the birthday wine on the table. But the oldest son-in-law, who knew that the third one had not attended school, wanted to embarrass him.

"It is far too tiresome," said he, "just to sit here drinking: let us have a drinking game. Each one of us must invent a verse, one that rhymes and makes sense, on the words: 'in the sky, on the earth, at the table, in the room;' and whoever cannot do so, must empty three glasses as a punishment."

All the company were satisfied. Only the third son-in-law felt embarrassed and insisted on leaving. But the guests would not let him go, and obliged him to keep his seat.

Then the oldest son-in-law began: "I will make a start with my verse. Here it is:

"In the sky the phoenix proudly flies,
On the earth the lambkin tamely lies,

At the table through an ancient book I wade,
In the room I softly call the maid."

The second one continued: "And I say:

"In the sky the turtle-dove flies round,
On the earth the ox paws up the ground,
At the table one studies the deeds of yore,
In the room the maid she sweeps the floor."

But the third son-in-law stuttered, and found nothing
to say. And when all of them insisted, he broke out in
rough tones of voice:

"In the sky—flies a leaden bullet,
On the earth—stalks a tiger-beast,
On the table—lies a pair of scissors,
In the room—I call the stable-boy."

On the earth our tiger-beast will devour your sheep and your ox.

The other two sons-in-law clapped their hands and began to laugh loudly.

"Why, the four lines do not rhyme at all," said they, "and besides, they do not make sense. A leaden bullet is no bird, the stable-boy does his work outside, would you call him into the room? Nonsense, nonsense! Drink!"

Yet before they had finished speaking, the third daughter raised the curtain of the women's room, and stepped out. She was angry, yet she could not suppress a smile.

"How so do our lines not make sense?" said she. "Listen a moment, and I'll explain them to you: In the sky our leaden bullet will shoot your phoenix and your turtle-dove. On the earth our tiger-beast will devour your sheep and your ox. On the table our pair of scissors will cut up all your old books. And finally, in the room—well, the stable-boy can marry your maid!"

Then the oldest son-in-law said: "Well scolded! Sister-in-law, you know how to talk! If you were a man you would have had your degree long ago. And, as a punishment, we will empty our three glasses."

The Bird with Nine Heads

LONG, LONG AGO, there once lived a king and a queen who had a daughter. One day, when the daughter went walking in the garden, a tremendous storm suddenly came up and carried her away with it. Now the storm had come from the bird with nine heads, who had robbed the princess, ad brought her to his cave. The king did not know whither his daughter had disappeared, so he had proclaimed throughout the land: "Whoever brings back the princess may have her for his bride!"

Now a youth had seen the bird as he was carrying the princess to his cave. This cave, though, was in the middle of a sheer wall of rock. One could not climb up to it from below, nor could one climb down to it from above. And as the youth was walking around the rock, another youth came along and asked him what he was doing there. So the first youth told him that the bird with nine heads had carried off the king's daughter, and had brought her up to his cave. The other chap knew what he had to do. He called together his friends, and they lowered the youth to the cave in a basket. And when he went into the cave, he saw the king's daughter sitting there, and washing the wound of the bird with nine heads; for the hound of heaven had bitten off his tenth head, and his wound was still bleeding. The princess, however, motioned to the youth to hide, and he did so.

When the king's daughter had washed his wound and bandaged it, the bird with nine heads felt so comfortable, that one after another, all his nine heads fell asleep. Then the youth stepped forth from his hiding-place, and cut off all nine heads with a sword. But the king's daughter said: "It would be best if you were hauled up first, and I came after."

"No," said the youth. "I will wait below here, until you are in safety." At first the king's daughter was not willing; yet at last she allowed herself to be persuaded, and climbed into the basket. But before she did so, she took a long pin from her hair, broke it into two halves, and gave him one and kept the other. She also divided her silken kerchief with him, and told him to take good care of both her gifts. But when the other man had drawn up the king's daughter, he took her along with him, and left the youth in the cave, in spite of all his calling and pleading.

The youth now took a walk about the cave. There he saw a number of maidens, all of whom had been carried off by the bird with nine heads, and who had perished there of hunger. And on the wall hung a fish, nailed against it with four nails. When he touched the fish, the latter turned into a handsome youth, who thanked him for delivering him, and they agreed to regard each other as brothers. Soon the first youth grew very hungry. He stepped out in front of the cave to search for food, but only stones were lying there. Then, suddenly, he saw a great dragon, who was licking a stone. The youth imitated him, and before long his hunger had disappeared. He next asked the dragon how he could get away from the cave, and the dragon nodded his head in the direction of his tail, as much as to say he should seat himself upon it. So he climbed up, and in the twinkling of an eye he was down on the ground, and the dragon had disappeared. He then went on until he found a tortoise-shell full of beautiful pearls. But they were magic pearls, for if you flung them into the fire, the fire ceased to burn, and if you flung them into the water, the water divided and you could walk through the midst of it. The youth took the pearls out of the tortoise-shell, and put them in his pocket. Not long after, he reached the sea-shore. Here he flung a pearl into the sea, and at once the waters divided and he could see the sea-dragon. The sea-dragon cried: "Who is disturbing me here in my own kingdom?" The youth answered: "I found pearls in a tortoise-shell, and have flung one into the sea, and now the waters have divided for me."

"If that is the case," said the dragon, "then come into the sea with me and we will live there together." Then the youth recognized him for the same dragon whom he had seen in the cave. And with him was the youth with whom he had formed a bond of brotherhood: He was the dragon's son.

"Since you have saved my son and become his brother, I am your father," said the old dragon. And he entertained him hospitably with food and wine.

One day his friend said to him: "My father is sure to want to reward you. But accept no money, nor any jewels from him, but only the little gourd flask over yonder. With it you can conjure up whatever you wish."

And, sure enough, the old dragon asked him what he wanted by way of a reward, and the youth answered: "I want no money, nor any jewels. All I want is the little gourd flask over yonder."

At first the dragon did not wish to give it up, but at last he did let him have it, after all. And then the youth left the dragon's castle.

When he set his foot on dry land again he felt hungry. At once a table stood before him, covered with a fine and

The youth left the dragon's castle.

plenteous meal. He ate and drank. After he had gone on
a while, he felt weary. And there stood an ass, waiting for
him, on which he mounted. After he had ridden for a
while, the ass's gait seemed too uneven, and along came
a wagon, into which he climbed. But the wagon shook
him up too, greatly, and he thought: "If I only had a litter!
That would suit me better." No more had he thought so,
than the litter came along, and he seated himself in it.
And the bearers carried him to the city in which dwelt
the king, the queen and their daughter.

When the other youth had brought back the king's daughter, it was decided to hold the wedding. But the king's daughter was not willing, and said: "He is not the right man. My deliverer will come and bring with him half of the long pin for my hair, and half my silken kerchief as a token." But when the youth did not appear for so long a time, and the other one pressed the king, the king grew impatient and said: "The wedding shall take place to-morrow!" Then the king's daughter went sadly through the streets of the city, and searched and searched in the hope of finding her deliverer. And this was on the very day that the litter arrived. The king's daughter saw the half of her silken handkerchief in the youth's hand, and filled with joy, she led him to her father. There he had to show his half of the long pin, which fitted the other exactly, and then the king was convinced that he was the right, true deliverer. The false bridegroom was now punished, the wedding celebrated, and they lived in peace and happiness till the end of their days.

Note: The long hair needle is an example of the halved jewel used as a sign of recognition by lovers. The "fish" in the cave is the dragon's son, for like East Indian *Nagaradjas,* the Chinese dragons are often sea-gods. Gourd flasks often occur as magic talismans in Chinese fairy-tales, and spirits who serve their owners are often imprisoned in them.

The Cave of the Beasts

O NCE UPON A TIME there was a family in which there were seven daughters. One day, when the father went out to gather wood, he found seven wild duck eggs. He brought them home, but did not think of giving any to his children, intending to eat them himself, with his wife. In the evening the oldest daughter woke up, and asked her mother what she was cooking. The mother said: "I am cooking wild duck eggs. I will give you one, but you must not let your sisters know." And so she gave her one. Then the second daughter woke up, and asked her mother what she was cooking. She said: "Wild duck eggs. If you will not tell your sisters, I'll give you one." And so it went. At last the daughters had eaten all the eggs, and there were none left.

In the morning the father was very angry with the children, and said: "Who wants to go along to grandmother?" But he intended to lead the children into the mountains, and let the wolves devour them there. The older daughters suspected this, and said: "We are not going along!" But the two younger ones said: "We will go with you." And so they drove off with their father. After they had driven a good ways, they asked: "Will we soon get to grandmother's house?" "Right away," said their father. And when they had reached the mountains he told them: "Wait here. I will drive into the village ahead of you, and tell grandmother that you are

13

coming." And then he drove off with the donkey-cart. They waited and waited, but their father did not come. At last they decided that their father would not come back to fetch them, and that he had left them alone in the mountains. So they went further and further into the hills seeking a shelter for the night. Then they spied a great stone. This they selected for a pillow, and rolled it over to the place where they were going to lie down to sleep. And then they saw that the stone was the door to a cave. There was a light in the cave, and they went into it. The light they had seen came from the many precious stones and jewels of every sort in the cave, which belonged to a wolf and a fox. They had a number of jars of precious stones and pearls that shone by night. The girls said: "What a lovely cave this is! We will lie right down and go to bed." For there stood two golden beds with gold-embroidered covers. So they lay down and fell asleep. During the night the wolf and fox came home. And the wolf said: "I smell human flesh!" But the fox replied: "Oh, nonsense! There are no human beings who can enter our cave. We lock it up too well for that." The wolf said: "Very well, then let us lie down in our beds and sleep." But the fox answered: "Let us curl up in the kettles on the hearth. They still hold a little warmth from the fire." The one kettle was of gold and the other of silver, and they curled up in them.

When the girls rose early in the morning, they saw the wolf and the fox lying there, and were much frightened. And they put the covers on the kettles and heaped a number of big stones on them, so that the wolf and the fox could not get out again. Then they made a fire. The wolf and the fox said: "Oh, how nice and warm it is this morning! How does that happen?" But at length it grew too hot for them. Then they noticed that the two girls had kindled a fire, and they cried: "Let us out! We will give you lots of precious stones, and lots of gold, and will do you no harm!" But the girls would not listen to them, and kept on making a bigger fire. So that was the end of the wolf and the fox in the kettles.

Then the girls lived happily for a number of days in the cave. But their father was seized with a longing for his daughters, and he went into the mountains to look for them. And he sat right down on the stone in front of the cave to rest, and tapped his pipe against it to empty the ashes. Then the girls within called out: "Who is knocking at our door?" And the father said: "Are those not my daughters' voices?" While the daughters replied: "Is that not our father's voice?" Then they pushed aside the stone and saw that it was their father, and their father was glad to see them once more. He was much surprised to think that they should have chanced on this cave full of precious stones, and they told him the whole story. Then their father fetched people to help him carry home the jewels. And when they got home, his wife wondered where he had obtained all these treasures. So the father and daughters told her everything, and they became a very wealthy family, and lived happily to the end of their days.

The Panther

ONCE UPON A TIME there was a widow who had two daughters and a little son. And one day the mother said to her daughters: "Take good care of the house, for I am going to see grandmother, together with your little brother!" So the daughters promised her they would do so, and their mother went off. On her way a panther met her, and asked where she was going.

"She said: "I am going with my child to see my mother."

"Will you not rest a bit?" asked the panther.

"No," said she, "It is already late, and it is a long road to where my mother lives."

But the panther did not cease urging her, and finally she gave in and sat down by the roadside.

"I will comb your hair a bit," said the panther. And the woman allowed the panther to comb her hair. But as he passed his claws through her hair, he tore off a bit of her skin and devoured it.

"Stop!" cried the woman. "The way you comb my hair hurts!"

But the panther tore off a much larger piece of skin. Now the woman wanted to call for help, but the panther seized and devoured her. Then he turned on her little son and killed him too, put on the woman's clothes, and laid the child's bones, which he had not yet devoured, in her basket. After that he went to the woman's home, where her two daughters were, and called in at the door: "Open the door, daughters! Mother has come home!" But they looked out through a crack and said: "Our mother's eyes are not so large as yours!"

Then the panther said: "I have been to grand-mother's house, and saw her hens laying eggs. That pleases me, and is the reason why my eyes have grown so large."

"Our mother had no spots in her face such as you have."

"Grandmother had no spare bed, so I had to sleep on the peas, and they pressed themselves into my face."

"Our mother's feet are not so large as yours."

"Stupid things! That comes from walking such a distance. Come, open the door quickly!"

Then the daughters said to each other: "It must be our mother," and they opened the door. But when the panther came in, they saw it was not really their mother after all.

At evening, when the daughters were already in bed, the panther was still gnawing the bones he had brought with him.

Then the daughters asked: "Mother, what are you eating?"

"I'm eating beets," was the answer.

Then the daughters said: "Oh, mother, give us some of your beets, too! We are so hungry!"

"No," was the reply, "I will not give you any. Now be quiet and go to sleep."

But the daughters kept on begging until the false mother gave them a little finger. And then they saw that it was their little brother's finger, and they said to each other: "We must make haste to escape else he will eat us as well." And with that they ran out of the door,

The daughters climbed up into a tree in the courtyard.

climbed up into a tree in the courtyard, and called down to the false mother: "Come out! We can see our neighbor's son celebrating his wedding!" But it was the middle of the night.

Then the mother came out, and when she saw that they were sitting in the tree, she called out angrily: "Why, I'm not able to climb!"

The daughters said: "Get into a basket and throw us the rope and we will draw you up!"

The mother did as they said. But when the basket was half-way up, they began to swing it back and forth, and bump it against the tree. Then the false mother had to turn into a panther again, lest she fall down. And the panther leaped out of the basket, and ran away.

Gradually daylight came. The daughters climbed down, seated themselves on the doorstep, and cried for their mother. And a needle-vender came by and asked them why they were crying.

"A panther has devoured our mother and our brother," said the girls. "He has gone now, but he is sure to return and devour us as well."

Then the needle-vender gave them a pair of needles, and said: "Stick these needles in the cushion of the arm-chair, with the points up." The girls thanked him and went on crying.

Soon a scorpion-catcher came by; and he asked them why they were crying. "A panther has devoured our mother and brother," said the girls. "He has gone now, but he is sure to return and devour us as well."

The man gave them a scorpion, and said: "Put it behind the hearth in the kitchen." The girls thanked him and went on crying.

Then an egg-seller came by and asked them why they were crying. "A panther has devoured our mother and our brother," said the girls. "He has gone now, but he is sure to return and devour us as well."

So he gave them an egg, and said: "Lay it beneath the ashes in the hearth." The girls thanked him and went on crying.

Then a dealer in turtles came by, and they told him their tale. He gave them a turtle, and said: "Put it in the water-barrel in the courtyard." And then a man came by who sold wooden clubs. He asked them why they were crying. And they told him the whole story. Then he gave them two wooden clubs, and said: "Hang them up over the door to the street." The girls thanked him and did as the men had told them.

To cool his hand the panther dipped it into the water-barrel.

In the evening the panther came home. He sat down in the armchair in the room. Then the needles in the cushion stuck into him. So he ran into the kitchen to light the fire and see what had jabbed him so; and then it was that the scorpion hooked his sting into his hand. And when at last the fire was burning, the egg burst and spurted into one of his eyes, which was blinded. So he ran out into the courtyard and dipped his hand into the water-barrel, in order to cool it; and then the turtle bit it off. And when in his pain he ran out through the door into the street, the wooden clubs fell on his head and that was the end of him.

Note: "The Panther" in this tale is made up of the same motives found in "Little Red Riding-Hood."

The Great Flood

ONCE UPON A TIME there was a widow, who had a child. And the child was a kind-hearted boy of whom everyone was fond. One day he said to his mother: "All the other children have a grandmother, but I have none. And that makes me feel very sad!"

"We will hunt up a grandmother for you," said his mother. Now it once happened that an old beggar-woman came to the house, who was very old and feeble. And when the child saw her, he said to her: "You shall be my grandmother!" And he went to his mother and said: "There is a beggar-woman outside, whom I want for my grandmother!" And his mother was willing and called her into the house; though the old woman was very dirty. So the boy said to his mother: "Come, let us wash grandmother!" And they washed the woman. But she had a great many burrs in her hair, so they picked them all out and put them in a jar, and they filled the whole jar. Then the grandmother said: "Do not throw them away, but bury them in the garden. And you must not dig them up again before the great flood comes."

"When is the great flood coming?" asked the boy.

"When the eyes of the two stone lions in front of the prison grow red, then the great flood will come," said the grandmother.

So the boy went to look at the lions, but their eyes

21

were not yet red. And the grandmother also said to him: "Make a little wooden ship and keep it in a little box." And this the boy did. And he ran to the prison every day and looked at the lions, much to the astonishment of the people in the street.

One day, as he passed the chicken-butcher's shop, the butcher asked him why he was always running to the lions. And the boy said: "When the lions' eyes grow red, then the great flood will come." But the butcher laughed at him. And the following morning, quite early, he took some chicken-blood and rubbed it on the lions' eyes. When the boy saw that the lions' eyes were red, he ran swiftly home and told his mother and grandmother. And then his grandmother said: "Dig up the jar quickly, and take the little ship out of its box." And when they dug up the jar, it was filled with the purest pearls; and the little ship grew larger and larger, like a real ship. Then the grandmother said: "Take the jar with you and get into the ship. And when the great flood comes, then you may save all the animals that are driven into it; but human beings, with their black heads, you are not to save." So they climbed into the ship, and the grandmother suddenly disappeared.

Now it began to rain, and the rain kept falling more and more heavily from the heavens. Finally there were no longer any single drops falling, but just one big sheet of water which flooded everything.

Then a dog came drifting along, and they saved him in their ship. Soon after came a pair of mice, with their little ones, loudly squeaking in their fear. And these they also saved. The water was already rising to the roofs of the houses, and on one roof stood a cat, arching her back and mewing pitifully. They took the cat into the ship, too. Yet the flood increased and rose to the tops of the trees. And in one tree sat a raven, beating his wings and cawing loudly. And him, too, they took in. Finally a swarm of bees came flying their way. The little creatures were quite wet, and could hardly fly. So they took in the bees on their ship. At last a man with black hair floated by on the waves. The boy said: "Mother, let us save him, too!" But the mother did not want to do so. "Did not grandmother tell us that we must save no black-headed human beings?" But the

The boy saw that the lion's eyes were red.

boy answered: "We will save the man in spite of that. I feel sorry for him, and cannot bear to see him drifting along in the water." So they also saved the man.

Gradually the water subsided. Then they got out of their ship, and parted from the man and the beasts. And the ship grew small again and they put it away in its box.

But the man was filled with a desire for the pearls. He went to the judge and entered a complaint against the boy and his mother, and they were both thrown into jail. Then the mice came, and dug a hole in the wall. And the dog came through the hole and brought them meat, and the cat brought them bread, so they did not have to hunger in their prison. But the raven flew off and returned with a letter for the judge. The letter had been written by a god, and it said: "I wandered about in the world of men disguised as a beggar woman. And this boy and his mother took me in. The boy treated me like his own grandmother, and did not shrink from washing me when I was dirty. Because of this I saved them out of the great flood by means of which I destroyed the sinful city wherein they dwelt. Do you, O judge, free them, or misfortune shall be your portion!"

So the judge had them brought before him, and asked what they had done, and how they had made their way through the flood. Then they told him everything, and what they said agreed with the god's letter. So the judge punished their accuser, and set them both at liberty.

When the boy had grown up he came to a city of many people, where it was said that the princess intended to take a husband. But in order to find the right man, she had veiled herself, and seated herself in a litter, and she had had the litter, together with many others, carried into the marketplace. In every litter sat a veiled woman, and the princess was in their midst. And whoever hit upon the right litter, he was to get the princess for his bride. So the youth went there, too, and when he reached the marketplace, he saw the bees whom he had saved from the great flood, all swarming about a certain litter. Up he stepped to it, and sure enough, the princess was sitting in it. And then their wedding was celebrated, and they lived happily ever afterward.

Why Dog and Cat Are Enemies

ONCE UPON A TIME there was a man and his wife, and they had a ring of gold. It was a lucky ring, and whoever owned it always had enough to live on. But this they did not know, and hence sold the ring for a small sum. But no sooner was the ring gone than they began to grow poorer and poorer, and at last did not know when they would get their next meal. They had a dog and a cat, and these had to go hungry as well. Then the two animals took counsel together as to how they might restore to their owners their former good fortune. At length the dog hit upon an idea.

"They must have the ring back again," he said to the cat.

The cat answered: "The ring has been carefully locked up in a chest, where no one can get at it."

"You must catch a mouse," said the dog, "and the mouse must gnaw a hole in the chest and fetch out the ring. And if she does not want to, say that you will bite her to death, and you will see that she will do it."

This advice pleased the cat, and she caught a mouse. Then she wanted to go to the house in which stood the chest, and the dog came after. They came to a broad river. And since the cat could not swim, the dog took her on his back and swam across with her. Then the cat carried the mouse to the house in which the chest stood. The mouse gnawed a hole in the chest, and

The mouse gnawed a hole in the chest, and fetched out the ring.

fetched out the ring. The cat put the ring in her mouth and went back to the river, where the dog was waiting for her, and swam across with her. Then they started out together for home, in order to bring the lucky ring to their master and mistress. But the dog could only run along the ground; when there was a house in the way he always had to go around it. The cat, however, quickly climbed over the roof, and so she reached home long before the dog, and brought the ring to her master.

Then her master said to his wife: "What a good creature the cat is! We will always give her enough to eat and care for her as though she were our own child!"

But when the dog came home they beat him and scolded him, because he had not helped to bring home the ring again. And the cat sat by the fireplace, purred, and said never a word. Then the dog grew angry at the cat, because she had robbed him of his reward, and when he saw her he chased her and tried to seize her.

And ever since that day cat and dog have been enemies.

The Herd Boy and the Weaving Maiden

T HE HERD BOY was the child of poor people. When he
was twelve years old, he took service with a farmer
to herd his cow. After a few years the cow had grown
large and fat, and her hair shone like yellow gold. She
must have been a cow of the gods.

One day while he had her out at pasture in the mountains, she suddenly began to speak to the Herd Boy in a
human voice, as follows: "This is the Seventh Day. Now
the White Jade Ruler has nine daughters, who bathe
this day in the Sea of Heaven. The seventh daughter is
beautiful and wise beyond all measure. She spins the
cloud-silk for the King and Queen of Heaven, and pre-
sides over the weaving which maidens do on earth. It is
for this reason she is called the Weaving Maiden. And if
you go and take away her clothes while she bathes, you
may become her husband and gain immortality."

"But she is up in Heaven," said the Herd Boy, "and
how can I get there?"

"I will carry you there," answered the yellow cow.

So the Herd Boy climbed on the cow's back. In a moment clouds began to stream out of her hoofs, and she
rose into the air. About his ears there was a whistling
like the sound of the wind, and they flew along as
swiftly as lightning. Suddenly the cow stopped.

"Now we are here," said she.

Then round about him the Herd Boy saw forests of chrysophrase and trees of jade. The grass was of jasper and the flowers of coral. In the midst of all this splendor lay a great, four-square sea, covering some five hundred acres. Its green waves rose and fell, and fishes with golden scales were swimming about in it. In addition there were countless magic birds who winged above it and sang. Even in the distance the Herd Boy could see the nine maidens in the water. They had all laid down their clothes on the shore.

"Take the red clothes, quickly," said the cow, "and hide away with them in the forest, and though she ask you for them ever so sweetly do not give them back to her until she has promised to become your wife."

Then the Herd Boy hastily got down from the cow's back, seized the red clothes and ran away. At the same moment the nine maidens noticed him and were much frightened.

"O youth, whence do you come, that you dare to take our clothes?" they cried. "Put them down again quickly!"

But the Herd Boy did not let what they said trouble him; but crouched down behind one of the jade trees. Then eight of the maidens hastily came ashore and drew on their clothes.

"Our seventh sister," said they, "whom Heaven has destined to be yours, has come to you. We will leave her alone with you."

The Weaving Maiden was still crouching in the water.

But the Herd Boy stood before her and laughed.

"If you will promise to be my wife," said he, "then I will give you your clothes."

But this did not suit the Weaving Maiden.

"I am a daughter of the Ruler of the Gods," said she, "and may not marry without his command. Give back

my clothes to me quickly, or else my father will punish you!"

Then the yellow cow said: "You have been destined
for each other by fate, and I will be glad to arrange your
marriage, and your father, the Ruler of the Gods, will
make no objection. Of that I am sure."

The Weaving Maiden replied: "You are an unreason-
ing animal! How could you arrange our marriage?"

The cow said: "Do you see that old willow-tree there
on the shore? Just give it a trial and ask it. If the willow
tree speaks, then Heaven wishes your union."

And the Weaving Maiden asked the willow.

The willow replied in a human voice:

> "This is the Seventh Day,
> The Herd Boy his court to the Weaver doth pay!"

and the Weaving Maiden was satisfied with the verdict.
The Herd Boy laid down her clothes, and went on
ahead. The Weaving Maiden drew them on and
followed him. And thus they became man and wife.

But after seven days she took leave of him.

"The Ruler of Heaven has ordered me to look after
my weaving," said she. "If I delay too long I fear that he
will punish me. Yet, although we have to part now, we
will meet again in spite of it."

When she had said these words she really went away.
The Herd Boy ran after her. But when he was quite near
she took one of the long needles from her hair and drew
a line with it right across the sky, and this line turned
into the Silver River. And thus they now stand, sepa-
rated by the river, and watch for one another.

And since that time they meet once every year, on
the eve of the Seventh Day. When that time comes, then
all the crows in the world of men come flying and form
a bridge over which the Weaving Maiden crosses the

*And since that time they meet once every year,
on the eve of the Seventh Day.*

Silver River. And on that day you will not see a single crow in the trees, from morning to night, no doubt because of the reason I have mentioned. And besides, a fine rain often falls on the evening of the Seventh Day. Then the women and old grandmothers say to one another: "Those are the tears which the Herd Boy and the Weaving Maiden shed at parting!" And for this reason the Seventh Day is a rain festival.

To the west of the Silver River is the constellation of the Weaving Maiden, consisting of three stars. And directly in front of it are three other stars in the form of a triangle. It is said that once the Herd Boy was angry because the Weaving Maiden had not wished to cross the Silver River, and had thrown his yoke at her, which fell down just in front of her feet. East of the Silver River is the Herd Boy's constellation, consisting of six stars. To one side of it are countless little stars which form a constellation pointed at both ends and somewhat broader in the middle. It is said that the Weaving Maiden in turn threw her spindle at the Herd Boy; but that she did not hit him, the spindle falling down to one side of him.

Note: "The Herd Boy and the Weaving Maiden" is retold after an oral source. The Herd Boy is a constellation in Aquila, the Weaving Maiden one in Lyra. The Silver River which separates them is the Milky Way. The Seventh Day of the seventh month is the festival of their reunion. The Ruler of the Heavens has nine daughters in all, who dwell in the nine heavens.

The Lady of the Moon

IN THE DAYS of the Emperor Yau lived a prince by the name of Hou I, who was a mighty hero and a good archer. Once ten suns rose together in the sky, and shone so brightly and burned so fiercely that the people on earth could not endure them. So the Emperor ordered Hou I to shoot at them. And Hou I shot nine of them down from the sky. Beside his bow, Hou I also had a horse which ran so swiftly that even the wind could not catch up with it. He mounted it to go a-hunting, and the horse ran away and could not be stopped. So Hou I came to Kunlun Mountain and met the Queen-Mother of the Jasper Sea. And she gave him the herb of immortality. He took it home with him and hid it in his room. But his wife, who was named Tschang O, once ate some of it on the sly when he was not at home, and she immediately floated up to the clouds. When she reached the moon, she ran into the castle there, and has lived there ever since as the Lady of the Moon.

On a night in mid-autumn, an emperor of the Tang dynasty once sat at wine with two sorcerers. And one of them took his bamboo staff and cast it into the air, where it turned into a heavenly bridge, on which the three climbed up to the moon together. There they saw a great castle on which was inscribed: "The Spreading Halls of Crystal Cold." Beside it stood a cassia tree

She has lived there ever since as the Lady of the Moon.

which blossomed and gave forth a fragrance filling all the air. And in the tree sat a man who was chopping off the smaller boughs with an ax. One of the sorcerers said: "That is the man in the moon. The cassia tree grows so luxuriantly that in the course of time it would overshadow all the moon's radiance. Therefore it has to be cut down once in every thousand years." Then they entered the spreading halls. The silver stories of the castle towered one above the other, and its walls and columns were all formed of liquid crystal. In the walls were cages and ponds, where fishes and birds moved as though alive. The whole moon-world seemed made of glass. While they were still looking about them on all sides the Lady of the Moon stepped up to them, clad in a white mantle and a rainbow-colored gown. She smiled and said to the emperor: "You are a prince of the mundane world of dust. Great is your fortune, since you have been able to find your way here!" And she called for her attendants, who came flying up on white birds, and sang and danced beneath the cassia tree. A pure clear music floated through the air. Beside the tree stood a mortar made of white marble, in which a jasper rabbit ground up herbs. That was the dark half of the moon. When the dance had ended, the emperor returned to earth again with the sorcerers. And he had the songs which he had heard on the moon written down and sung to the accompaniment of flutes of jasper in his pear-tree garden.

Note: This fairy tale is traditional. The archer Hou I is placed by legend in different epochs. He also occurs in connection with the myths regarding the moon, for one tale recounts how he saved the moon during an eclipse by means of his arrows. The Queen-Mother is Si Wang Mu. The Tang dynasty reigned A.D. 618–906. "The Spreading Halls of Crystal Cold": The goddess of the ice also has her habitation in the moon. The rabbit in the moon is a favorite figure. He grinds the grains of maturity or the herbs that make the elixir of life. The rain-toad Tschan, who has three legs, is also placed on the moon. According to one version of the story, Tschang O took the shape of this toad.

The Miserly Farmer

ONCE UPON A TIME there was a farmer who had carted pears to market. Since they were very sweet and fragrant, he hoped to get a good price for them. A bonze (monk) with a torn cap and tattered robe stepped up to his cart and asked for one. The farmer repulsed him, but the bonze did not go. Then the farmer grew angry and began to call him names. The bonze said: "You have pears by the hundred in your cart. I only ask for one. Surely that does you no great injury. Why suddenly grow so angry about it?"

The bystanders told the farmer that he ought to give the bonze one of the smaller pears and let him go. But the farmer would not and did not. An artisan saw the whole affair from his shop, and since the noise annoyed him, he took some money, bought a pear, and gave it to the bonze.

The bonze thanked him and said: "One like myself, who has given up the world, must not be miserly. I have beautiful pears myself, and I invite you all to eat them with me." Then some one asked: "If you have pears then why do you not eat your own?" He answered: "I first must have a seed to plant."

And with that he began to eat the pear with gusto. When he had finished, he held the pit in his hand, took his pick-ax from his shoulder, and dug a hole a couple of inches deep. Into this he thrust the pit, and covered it with earth. Then he asked the folk in the marketplace for water, with which to water it. A pair of curiosity seekers brought him hot water from the hostlery in the street, and with it the bonze watered the pit. Thousands of eyes were turned on the spot. And the pit could already be seen to sprout. The sprout grew and in a moment it had turned into a tree. Branches and leaves burgeoned out from it. It began to blossom and soon the fruit had ripened: large, fragrant pears, which hung in thick clusters from the boughs. The bonze climbed into the tree and handed down the pears to the bystanders. In a moment all the pears had been eaten up. Then the bonze took his pick-ax and cut down the tree. Crash, crash! so it went for a while, and the tree was felled. Then he took the tree on his shoulder and walked away at an easy gait.

When the bonze had begun to make his magic, the farmer, too, had mingled with the crowd. With neck outstretched and staring eyes he had stood there and had entirely forgotten the business he hoped to do with his pears. When the bonze had gone off he turned around to look after his cart. His pears had all disappeared. Then he realized that the pears the bonze had divided had been his own. He looked more closely, and the axle of his cart had disappeared. It was plainly evident that it had been chopped off quite recently. The farmer fell into a rage and hastened after the bonze as fast as ever he could. And when he turned the corner, there lay the missing piece from the axle by the city wall. And then he realized that the pear-tree which the bonze had chopped down must have been his axle. The bonze, however, was nowhere to be found. And the whole crowd in the market burst out into loud laughter.

Note: The axle in China is really a handle, for the little Chinese carts are one-wheel pushcarts with two handles or shafts.

Old Dschang

O NCE UPON A TIME there was a man who went by the name of Old Dschang. He lived in the country, near Yangdschou, as a gardener. His neighbor, named Sir We, held an official position in Yangdschou. Sir We had decided that it was time for his daughter to marry, so he sent for a match-maker and commissioned her to find a suitable husband. Old Dschang heard this, and was pleased. He prepared food and drink, entertained the match-maker, and told her to recommend him as a husband. But the old match-maker went off scolding.

The next day he invited her to dinner again and gave her money. Then the old match-maker said: "You do not know what you wish! Why should a gentleman's beautiful daughter condescend to marry a poor old gardener like yourself? Even though you had money to burn, your white hair would not match her black locks. Such a marriage is out of the question!"

But Old Dschang did not cease to entreat her: "Make an attempt, just one attempt, to mention me! If they will not listen to you, then I must resign myself to my fate!"

The old match-maker had taken his money, so she could not well refuse, and though she feared being scolded, she mentioned him to Sir We. He grew angry and wanted to throw her out of the house.

"I knew you would not thank me," said she, "but the old man urged it so that I could not refuse to mention his intention."

Sir We's daughter was married to Old Dschang.

"Tell the old man that if this very day he brings me two white jade-stones, and four hundred ounces of yellow gold, then I will give him my daughter's hand in marriage."

But he only wished to mock the old man's folly, for he knew that the latter could not give him anything of the kind. The match-maker went to Old Dschang and delivered the message. And he made no objection; but at once brought the exact quantity of gold and jewels to Sir We's house. The latter was very much frightened and when his wife heard of it, she began to weep and wail loudly. But the girl encouraged her mother: "My father has given his word now and cannot break it. I will know how to bear my fate."

So Sir We's daughter was married to Old Dschang. But even after the wedding the latter did not give up his work as a gardener. He spaded the field and sold vegetables as usual, and his wife had to fetch water and build the kitchen fire herself. But she did her work without false shame and, though her relatives reproached her, she continued to do so.

Once an aristocratic relative visited Sir We and said: "If you had really been poor, were there not enough young gentlemen in the neighborhood for your daughter? Why did you have to marry her to such a wrinkled old gardener? Now that you have thrown her away, so to speak, it would be better if both of them left this part of the country."

Then Sir We prepared a banquet and invited his daughter and Old Dschang to visit him. When they had had sufficient to eat and drink he allowed them to get an inkling of what was in his mind.

Said Old Dschang: "I have only remained here because I thought you would long for your daughter. But since you are tired of us, I will be glad to go. I have a little country house back in the hills, and we will set out for it early tomorrow morning."

The following morning, at break of dawn, Old Dschang came with his wife to say farewell. Sir We said: "Should we long to see you at some later time, my son can make inquiries." Old Dschang placed his wife on a donkey and gave her a straw hat to wear. He himself took his staff and walked after.

A few years passed without any news from either of them. Then Sir We and his wife felt quite a longing to see their daughter and sent their son to make inquiries. When the latter got back in the hills he met a plow-boy who was plowing with two yellow steers. He asked him: "Where is Old Dschang's country house?" The plow-boy left the plow in the harrow, bowed and answered: "You have been a long time coming, sir! The village is not far from here; I will show you the way."

They crossed a hill. At the foot of the hill flowed a brook, and when they had crossed the brook they had to climb another hill. Gradually the landscape changed. From the top of the hill could be seen a valley, level in the middle, surrounded by abrupt crags and shaded by green trees, among which houses and towers peeped forth. This was the country house of Old Dschang. Before the village flowed a deep brook full of clear, blue water. They passed over a stone bridge and reached the gate. Here flowers and trees grew in luxurious profusion, and peacocks and cranes flew about. From the distance could be heard the sound of flutes and of stringed instruments. Crystal-clear tones rose to the clouds. A messenger in a purple robe received the guest at the gate and led him into a hall of surpassing splendor. Strange fragrances filled the air, and there was a ringing of little bells of pearl. Two maid-servants came forth to greet him, followed by two rows of beautiful girls in a long processional. After them a man in a flowing turban, clad in scarlet silk, with red slippers, came floating along. The guest saluted him. He was serious and dignified, and at the same time seemed youthfully fresh. At first We's son did not recognize him, but when he looked more closely, why it was Old Dschang! The latter said with a smile: "I am pleased that the long road to travel has not prevented your coming. Your sister is just combing her hair. She will welcome you in a moment." Then he had him sit down and drink tea.

After a short time a maid-servant came and led him to the inner rooms, to his sister. The beams of her room were of sandalwood, the doors of tortoise-shell and the windows inlaid with blue jade; her curtains were formed of strings of pearls and the steps leading into the room of green nephrite. His sister was magnificently gowned, and far more beautiful than before. She asked him carelessly how he was getting along, and what her parents were doing; but was not very cordial. After a splendid meal she had an apartment prepared for him.

"My sister wishes to make an excursion to the Mountain of the Fairies," said Old Dschang to him. "We will be back about sunset, and you can rest until we return."

Then many-colored clouds rose in the courtyard, and dulcet music sounded on the air. Old Dschang mounted a dragon, while his wife and sister rode on phoenixes and their attendants on cranes. So they rose into the air and disappeared in an easterly direction. They did not return until after sunset.

Old Dschang and his wife then said to him: "This is an abode of the blessed. You cannot remain here overlong. To-morrow we will escort you back."

On the following day, when taking leave, Old Dschang gave him eighty ounces of gold and an old straw hat. "Should you need money," said he, "you can go to Yangdschou and inquire in the northern suburb for Old Wang's drug-shop. There you can collect ten million pieces of copper. This hat is the order for them." Then he ordered his plow-boy to take him home again.

Quite a few of the folks at home, to whom he described his adventures, thought that Old Dschang must be a holy man, while others regarded the whole thing as a magic vision.

After five or six years Sir We's money came to an end. So his son took the straw hat to Yangdschou and there asked for Old Wang. The latter just happened to be standing in his drug-shop, mixing herbs. When the son explained his errand he said: "The money is ready. But is your hat genuine?" And he took the hat and examined it. A young girl came from an inner room and said: "I wove the hat for Old Dschang myself. There must be a red thread in it." And sure enough, there was. Then Old Wang gave Young We the ten million pieces of copper, and the latter now believed that Old Dschang was really a saint. So he once more went over the hills to look for him. He asked the forest-keepers, but they could tell him naught. Sadly he retraced his steps and decided to inquire of Old Wang, but he had also disappeared.

When several years had passed he once more came to Yangdschou, and was walking in the meadow before the city gate. There he met Old Dschang's plow-boy. The latter cried out: "How are you? How are you?" and drew out ten pounds of gold, which he gave to him, saying: "My mistress told me to give you this. My master is this very moment drinking tea with Old Wang in the inn." Young We followed the plow-boy, intending to greet his brother-in-law. But when he reached the inn there was no one in sight. And when he turned around the plow-boy had disappeared as well. And since that time no one ever heard from Old Dschang again.

Note: The match-maker, according to Chinese custom—and the custom of other Asian peoples—is an absolutely necessary mediator between the two families.

The Flower-Elves

ONCE UPON A TIME there was a scholar who lived retired from the world in order to gain hidden wisdom. He lived alone and in a secret place. And all about the little house in which he dwelt he had planted every kind of flower, and bamboos and other trees. There it lay, quite concealed in its thick grove of flowers. With him he had only a boy servant, who dwelt in a separate hut, and who carried out his orders. He was not allowed to appear before his master unless summoned. The scholar loved his flowers as he did himself. Never did he set his foot beyond the boundaries of his garden.

It chanced that once there came a lovely spring evening. Flowers and trees stood in full bloom, a fresh breeze was blowing, the moon shone clearly. And the scholar sat over his goblet and was grateful for the gift of life.

Suddenly he saw a maiden in dark garments come tripping up in the moonlight. She made a deep curtsy, greeted him and said: "I am your neighbor. We are a company of young maids who are on our way to visit the eighteen aunts. We should like to rest in this court for awhile, and therefore ask your permission to do so."

The scholar saw that this was something quite out of the common, and gladly gave his consent. The maiden thanked him and went away.

In a short time she brought back a whole crowd of

43

maids carrying flowers and willow branches. All greeted the scholar. They were charming, with delicate features, and slender, graceful figures. When they moved their sleeves, a delightful fragrance was exhaled. There is no fragrance known to the human world which could be compared with it.

The scholar invited them to sit down for a time in his room. Then he asked them: "Whom have I really the honor of entertaining? Have you come from the castle of the Lady of the Moon, or the Jade Spring of the Queen-Mother of the West?"

"How could we claim such high descent?" said a maiden in a green gown, with a smile. "My name is Salix." Then she presented another, clad in white, and said: "This is Mistress Prunophora"; then one in rose, "and this is Persica"; and finally one in a dark-red gown, "and this is Punica. We are all sisters and we want to visit the eighteen zephyr-aunts to-day. The moon shines so beautifully this evening and it is so charming here in the garden. We are most grateful to you for taking pity on us."

"Yes, yes," said the scholar.

Then the sober-clad servant suddenly announced: "The zephyr-aunts have already arrived!"

At once the girls rose and went to the door to meet them.

"We were just about to visit you, aunts," they said, smiling. "This gentleman here had just invited us to sit for a moment. What a pleasant coincidence that you aunts have come here, too. This is such a lovely night that we must drink a goblet of nectar in honor of you aunts!"

Thereon they ordered the servant to bring what was needed.

"May one sit down here?" asked the aunts.

They were charming, with delicate features,
and slender, graceful figures.

"The master of the house is most kind," replied the maids, "and the spot is quiet and hidden."

And then they presented the aunts to the scholar. He spoke a few kindly words to the eighteen aunts. They had a somewhat irresponsible and airy manner. Their words fairly gushed out, and in their neighborhood one felt a frosty chill.

Meanwhile the servants had already brought in table and chairs. The eighteen aunts sat at the upper end of the board, the maids followed, and the scholar sat down with them at the lowest place. Soon the entire table was covered with the most delicious foods and most magnificent fruits, and the goblets were filled with a fragrant nectar. They were delights such as the world of men does not know! The moon shone brightly and the flowers exhaled intoxicating odors. After they had partaken of food and drink the maids rose, danced and sung. Sweetly the sound of their singing echoed through the falling gloam, and their dance was like that of butterflies fluttering about the flowers. The scholar was so overpowered with delight that he no longer knew whether he was in heaven or on earth.

When the dance had ended, the girls sat down again at the table, and drank the health of the aunts in flowing nectar. The scholar, too, was remembered with a toast, to which he replied with well-turned phrases.

But the eighteen aunts were somewhat irresponsible in their ways. One of them, raising her goblet, by accident poured some nectar on Punica's dress. Punica, who was young and fiery, and very neat, stood up angrily when she saw the spot on her red dress.

"You are really very careless," said she, in her anger. "My other sisters may be afraid of you, but I am not!"

Then the aunts grew angry as well and said: "How dare this young chit insult us in such a manner!"

And with that they gathered up their garments and rose.

All the maids then crowded about them and said: "Punica is so young and inexperienced! You must not bear her any ill-will! To-morrow she shall go to you, switch in hand, and receive her punishment!"

But the eighteen aunts would not listen to them and went off. Thereupon the maids also said farewell, scattered among the flower-beds and disappeared. The scholar sat for a long time lost in dreamy yearning.

On the following evening the maids all came back again.

"We all live in your garden," they told him. "Every year we are tormented by naughty winds, and therefore we have always asked the eighteen aunts to protect us. But yesterday Punica insulted them, and now we fear they will help us no more. But we know that you have always been well disposed toward us, for which we are heartily grateful. And now we have a great favor to ask, that every New Year's Day you make a small scarlet flag, paint the sun, moon and five planets on it, and set it up in the eastern part of the garden. Then we sisters will be left in peace and will be protected from all evil. But since New Year's Day has passed for this year, we beg that you will set up the flag on the twenty-first of this month. For the East Wind is coming and the flag will protect us against him!"

The scholar readily promised to do as they wished, and the maids all said with a single voice: "We thank you for your great kindness and will repay it!" Then they departed and a sweet fragrance filled the entire garden.

The scholar, however, made a red flag as described, and when early in the morning of the day in question the East Wind really did begin to blow, he quickly set it up in the garden.

Suddenly a wild storm broke out, one that caused the forests to bend, and broke the trees. The flowers in the garden alone did not move.

Then the scholar noticed that Salix was the willow; Prunophora the plum; Persica the peach; and the saucy Punica the Pomegranate, whose powerful blossoms the wind cannot tear. The eighteen zephyr-aunts, however, were the spirits of the winds.

In the evening the flower-elves all came and brought the scholar radiant flowers as a gift of thanks.

"You have saved us," they said, "and we have nothing

The scholar ate the flowers, and he grew young again.

else we can give you. If you eat these flowers you will live long and avoid old age. And if you, in turn, will protect us every year, then we sisters, too, will live long."

The scholar did as they told him and ate the flowers. And his figure changed and he grew young again like a youth of twenty. And in the course of time he attained the hidden wisdom and was placed among the Immortals.

Note: Salix: the names of the "Flower-Elves" are given in the Chinese as family names, whose sound suggests the flower-names without exactly using them. In the translation the play on words is indicated by the Latin names. "Zephyr-aunts": in Chinese the name given the aunts is "Fong," which in another stylization means "wind."

The Dragon-Princess

I N THE SEA OF DUNGTING there is a hill, and in that hill
there is a hole, and this hole is so deep that it has
no bottom.

Once a fisherman was passing there who slipped and
fell into the hole. He came to a country full of winding
ways which led over hill and dale for several miles.
Finally he reached a dragon-castle lying in a great plain.
There grew a green slime which reached to his knees.
He went to the gate of the castle. It was guarded by a
dragon who spouted water which dispersed in a fine
mist. Within the gate lay a small hornless dragon who
raised his head, showed his claws, and would not let
him in.

The fisherman spent several days in the cave, satis-
fying his hunger with the green slime, which he found
edible and which tasted like rice-mush. At last he found
a way out again. He told the district mandarin what had
happened to him, and the latter reported the matter to
the emperor. The emperor sent for a wise man and
questioned him concerning it.

The wise man said: "There are four paths in this cave.
One path leads to the southwest shore of the Sea of
Dungting, the second path leads to a valley in the land
of the four rivers, the third path ends in a cave on the
mountain of Lo-Fu and the fourth in an island of the
Eastern Sea. In this cave dwells the seventh daughter of

the Dragon-King of the Eastern Sea, who guards his pearls and his treasure. It happened once in the ancient days, that a fisherboy dived into the water and brought up a pearl from beneath the chin of a black dragon. The dragon was asleep, which was the reason the fisherboy brought the pearl to the surface without being harmed. The treasure which the daughter of the Dragon-King has in charge is made up of thousands and millions of such jewels. Several thousands of small dragons watch over them in her service. Dragons have the peculiarity of avoiding wax. But they are fond of beautiful jade-stones, and of kung-tsing, the hollowgreen wood, and like to eat swallows. If one were to send a messenger with a letter, it would be possible to obtain precious pearls."

The emperor was greatly pleased, and announced a large reward for the man who was competent to go to the dragon-castle as his messenger.

In this cave dwells the seventh daughter
of the Dragon-King of the Eastern Sea.

The first man to come forward was named So Pi-Lo. But the wise man said: "A great-great-great-great-grand-father of yours once slew more than a hundred of the dragons of the Eastern Sea, and was finally himself slain by the dragons. The dragons are the enemies of your family and you cannot go."

Then came a man from Canton, Lo-Dsi-Tschun, with his two brothers, who said that his ancestors had been related to the Dragon-King. Hence they were well-liked by the dragons and well-known to them. They begged to be entrusted with the message.

The wise man asked: "And have you still in your pos-session the stone which compels the dragons to do your will?"

"Yes," said they, "we have brought it along with us."

The wise man had them show him the stone; then he spoke: "This stone is only obeyed by the dragons who make clouds and send down the rain. It will not do for the dragons who guard the pearls of the sea-king." Then he questioned them further: "Have you the dragon-brain vapor?"

When they admitted that they had not, the wise man said: "How then will you compel the dragons to yield their treasure?"

And the emperor said: "What shall we do?"

The wise man replied: "On the Western Ocean sail foreign merchants who deal in dragon-brain vapor. Someone must go to them and seek it from them. I also know a holy man who is an adept in the art of taming dragons, and who has prepared ten pounds of the dragon-stone. Someone should be sent for that as well."

The emperor sent out his messengers. They met one of the holy man's disciples and obtained two fragments of dragon-stone from him.

Said the wise man: "That is what we want!"

Several more months went by, and at last a pill of dragon-brain vapor had also been secured. The emperor felt much pleased and had his jewelers carve two little boxes of the finest jade. These were polished with the ashes of the Wutung-tree. And he had an essence prepared of the very best hollowgreen wood, pasted with sea-fish lime, and hardened in the fire. Of this two vases were made. Then the bodies and the clothing of the messengers were rubbed with tree-wax, and they were given five hundred roasted swallows to take along with them.

They went into the cave. When they reached the dragon-castle, the little dragon who guarded the gate smelled the tree-wax, so he crouched down and did them no harm. They gave him a hundred roasted swallows as a bribe to announce them to the daughter of the Dragon-King. They were admitted to her presence and offered her the jade caskets, the vases and the four hundred roasted swallows as gifts. The dragon's daughter received them graciously, and they unfolded the emperor's letter.

In the castle there was a dragon who was over a thousand years old. He could turn himself into a human being, and could interpret the language of human beings. Through him the dragon's daughter learned that the emperor was sending her the gifts, and she returned them with a gift of three great pearls, seven smaller pearls and a whole bushel of ordinary pearls. The messengers took leave, rode off with their pearls on a dragon's back, and in a moment they had reached the banks of the Yangtze-kiang. They made their way to Nanking, the imperial capital, and there handed over their treasure of gems.

The emperor was much pleased and showed them to the wise man. He said: "Of the three great pearls, one is a divine wishing-pearl of the third class, and two are

They made their way to Nanking, the imperial capital.

black dragon-pearls of medium quality. Of the seven smaller pearls two are serpent-pearls, and five are mussel-pearls. The remaining pearls are in part sea-crane pearls, in part snail and oyster-pearls. They do not approach the great pearls in value, and yet few will be found to equal them on earth."

The emperor also showed them to all his servants. They, however, thought the wise man's words all talk, and did not believe what he said.

Then the wise man said: "The radiance of wishing-pearls of the first class is visible for forty miles, that of the second class for twenty miles, and that of the third for ten miles. As far as their radiance carries, neither wind nor rain, thunder nor lightning, water, fire nor weapons may reach. The pearls of the black dragon are nine-colored and glow by night. Within the circle of their light the poison of serpents and worms is powerless. The serpent-pearls are seven-colored, the mussel-pearls five-colored. Both shine by night. Those most free from spots are the best. They grow within the mussel, and increase and decrease in size as the moon waxes and wanes."

Some one asked how the serpent- and sea-crane pearls could be told apart, and the wise man answered: "The animals themselves recognize them."

Then the emperor selected a serpent-pearl and a sea-crane pearl, put them together with a whole bushel of ordinary pearls, and poured the lot out in the court-yard. Then a large yellow serpent and a black crane were fetched and placed among the pearls. At once the crane took up a sea-crane pearl in his bill and began to dance and sing and flutter around. But the serpent snatched at the serpent-pearl, and wound himself about it in many coils. And when the people saw this they acknowledged the truth of the wise man's words. As regards the radiance of the larger and smaller pearls it turned out, too, just as the wise man had said.

In the dragon-castle the messengers had enjoyed dainty fare, which tasted like flowers, herbs, ointment and sugar. They had brought a remnant of it with them to the capital; yet exposed to the air it had become as hard as stone. The emperor commanded that these fragments be preserved in the treasury. Then he bestowed high rank and titles on the three brothers, and made each one of them a present of a thousand rolls of fine silk stuff. He also had investigated why it was that the fisherman, when he chanced upon the cave, had not been destroyed by the dragons. And it turned out that his fishing clothes had been soaked in oil and tree-wax. The dragons had dreaded the odor.

The Disowned Princess

A T THE TIME that the Tang dynasty was reigning there lived a man named Liu I, who had failed to pass his examinations for the doctorate. So he traveled home again. He had gone six or seven miles when a bird flew up in a field, and his horse shied and ran ten miles before he could stop him. There he saw a woman who was herding sheep on a hillside. He looked at her and she was lovely to look upon, yet her face bore traces of hidden grief. Astonished, he asked her what was the matter.

The woman began to sob and said: "Fortune has forsaken me, and I am in need and ashamed. Since you are kind enough to ask I will tell you all. I am the youngest daughter of the Dragon-King of the Sea of Dungting, and was married to the second son of the Dragon-King of Ging Dschou. Yet my husband ill-treated and disowned me. I complained to my step-parents, but they loved their son blindly and did nothing. And when I grew insistent they both became angry, and I was sent out here to herd sheep." When she had done, the woman burst into tears and lost all control of herself. Then she continued: "The Sea of Dungting is far from here; yet I know that you will have to pass it on your homeward journey. I should like to give you a letter to my father, but I do not know whether you would take it."

Liu I answered: "Your words have moved my heart.

Would that I had wings and could fly away with you. I will be glad to deliver the letter to your father. Yet the Sea of Dungting is long and broad, and how am I to find him?"

"On the southern shore of the Sea stands an orange-tree," answered the woman, "which people call the tree of sacrifice. When you get there you must loosen your girdle and strike the tree with it three times in succession. Then some one will appear whom you must follow. When you see my father, tell him in what need you found me, and that I long greatly for his help."

Then she fetched out a letter from her breast and gave it to Liu I. She bowed to him, looked toward the east and sighed, and, unexpectedly, the sudden tears rolled from the eyes of Liu I as well. He took the letter and thrust it in his bag.

Then he asked her: "I cannot understand why you have to herd sheep. Do the gods slaughter cattle like men?"

"These are not ordinary sheep," answered the woman; "these are rain-sheep."

"But what are rain-sheep?"

"They are the thunder-rams," replied the woman.

And when he looked more closely he noticed that these sheep walked around in proud, savage fashion, quite different from ordinary sheep.

Liu I added: "But if I deliver the letter for you, and you succeed in getting back to the Sea of Dungting in safety, then you must not use me like a stranger."

The woman answered: "How could I use you as a stranger? You shall be my dearest friend."

And with these words they parted.

In course of a month Liu I reached the Sea of Dungting, asked for the orange-tree and, sure enough, found it. He loosened his girdle, and struck the tree with it three times. At once a warrior emerged from the waves of the sea, and asked: "Whence come you, honored guest?"

Liu I said: "I have come on an important mission and want to see the King."

The warrior made a gesture in the direction of the water, and the waves turned into a solid street along which he led Liu I. The dragon-castle rose before them with its thousand gates, and magic flowers and rare grasses bloomed in luxurious profusion. The warrior bade him wait at the side of a great hall.

Liu I asked: "What is this place called?"

"It is the Hall of the Spirits," was the reply.

Liu I looked about him: all the jewels known to earth

A warrior emerged from the waves of the sea.

were there in abundance. The columns were of white quartz, inlaid with green jade; the seats were made of coral, the curtains of mountain crystal as clear as water, the windows of burnished glass, adorned with rich lattice-work. The beams of the ceiling, ornamented with amber, rose in wide arches. An exotic fragrance filled the hall, whose outlines were lost in darkness.

Liu I had waited for the king a long time. To all his questions the warrior replied: "Our master is pleased at this moment to talk with the priest of the sun up on the coral-tower about the sacred book of the fire. He will, no doubt, soon be through."

Liu I went on to ask: "Why is he interested in the sacred book of the fire?"

The reply was: "Our master is a dragon. The dragons are powerful through the power of water. They can cover hill and dale with a single wave. The priest is a human being. Human beings are powerful through fire. They can burn the greatest palaces by means of a torch. Fire and water fight each other, being different in their nature. For that reason our master is now talking with the priest, in order to find a way in which fire and water may complete each other."

Before they had quite finished there appeared a man in a purple robe, bearing a scepter of jade in his hand.

The warrior said: "This is my master!"

Liu I bowed before him.

The king asked: "Are you not a living human being? What has brought you here?"

Liu I gave his name and explained: "I have been to the capital and there failed to pass my examination. When I was passing by the Ging Dschou River, I saw your daughter, whom you love, herding sheep in the wilderness. The winds tousled her hair, and the rain drenched her. I could not bear to see her trouble and spoke to her. She complained that her husband had cast her out and wept bitterly. Then she gave me a letter for you. And that is why I have come to visit you, O King!"

With these words he fetched out his letter and handed it to the king. When the latter had read it, he hid his face in his sleeve and said with a sigh: "It is my own fault. I picked out a worthless husband for her. Instead of securing her happiness I have brought her to shame in a distant land. You are a stranger and yet you have been willing to help her in her distress, for which I am very grateful to you." Then he once more began to sob, and all those about him shed tears. Thereupon the monarch gave the letter to a servant who took it into the interior of the palace; and soon the sound of loud lamentations rose from the inner rooms.

The king was alarmed and turned to an official: "Go and tell them within not to weep so loudly! I am afraid that Tsian Tang may hear them."

"Who is Tsian Tang?" asked Liu I.

"He is my beloved brother," answered the king. "Formerly he was the ruler of the Tsian-Tang River, but now he has been deposed."

Liu I asked: "Why should the matter be kept from him?"

"He is so wild and uncontrollable," was the reply, "that I fear he would cause great damage. The deluge which covered the earth for nine long years in the time of the Emperor Yau was the work of his anger. Because he fell out with one of the kings of heaven, he caused a great deluge that rose and covered the tops of five high mountains. Then the king of heaven grew angry with him, and gave him to me to guard. I had to chain him to a column in my palace."

Before he had finished speaking a tremendous turmoil arose, which split the skies and made the earth tremble, so that the whole palace began to rock, and smoke and clouds rose hissing and puffing. A red dragon, a thousand feet long, with flashing eyes, blood-red tongue, scarlet scales and a fiery beard came surging up. He was dragging along through the air the column to which he had been bound, together with its chain. Thunders and lightnings roared and darted around his body; sleet and snow, rain and hail-stones whirled about him in confusion. There was a crash of thunder, and he flew up to the skies and disappeared.

Liu I fell to earth in terror. The king helped him up with his own hand and said: "Do not be afraid! That is my brother, who is hastening to Ging Dschou in his rage. We will soon have good news!"

Then he had food and drink brought in for his guest. When the goblet had thrice made the rounds, a gentle breeze began to murmur and a fine rain fell. A youth clad in a purple gown and wearing a lofty hat entered. A sword hung at his side. His appearance was manly and heroic. Behind him walked a girl radiantly beautiful, wearing a robe of misty fragrance. And when Liu I looked at her, lo, it was the dragon-princess whom he had met on his way! A throng of maidens in rosy garments received her, laughing and giggling, and led her into the interior of the palace. The king, however, presented Liu I to the youth and said: "This is Tsian Tang, my brother!"

Tsian Tang thanked him for having brought the message. Then he turned to his brother and said: "I have fought against the accursed dragons and have utterly defeated them!"

"How many did you slay?"

"Six hundred thousand."

"Were any fields damaged?"

"The fields were damaged for eight hundred miles around."

"And where is the heartless husband?"

"I ate him alive!"

Then the king was alarmed and said: "What the fickle boy did was not to be endured, it is true. But still you were a little too rough with him; in future you must not do anything of the sort again." And Tsian Tang promised not to.

That evening Liu I was feasted at the castle. Music and dancing lent charm to the banquet. A thousand warriors with banners and spears in their hands stood at attention. Trombones and trumpets resounded, and drums and kettledrums thundered and rattled as the warriors danced a war-dance. The music expressed how Tsian Tang had broken through the ranks of the enemy, and the hair of the guest who listened to it rose on his head in terror. Then, again, there was heard the music of strings, flutes and little golden bells. A thousand maidens in crimson and green silk danced around. The return of the princess was also told in tones. The music sounded like a song of sadness and plaining, and all who heard it were moved to tears. The King of the Sea of Dungting was filled with joy. He raised his goblet and drank to the health of his guest, and all sorrow departed from them. Both rulers thanked Liu I in verses, and Liu I answered them in a rhymed toast. The crowd of courtiers in the palace-hall applauded. Then the King of the Sea of Dungting drew forth a blue cloud-basket in which was the horn of a rhinoceros, which divides the water. Tsian Tang brought out a platter of red amber on which lay a carbuncle. These they presented to their guest, and the other inmates of the palace also heaped up embroideries, brocades and pearls by his side. Surrounded by shimmer and light Liu I sat there, smiling, and bowed his thanks to all sides. When the banquet was ended he slept in the Palace of Frozen Radiance.

On the following day another banquet was held. Tsian Tang, who was not quite himself, sat carelessly on his seat and said: "The Princess of the Dungting Sea is handsome and delicately fashioned. She has had the misfortune to be disowned by her husband, and to-day her marriage is annulled. I should like to find another husband for her. If you were agreeable it would be to your advantage. But if you were not willing to marry her, you may go your way, and should we ever meet again we will not know each other."

Liu I was angered by the careless way in which Tsian Tang spoke to him. The blood rose to his head and he replied: "I served as a messenger, because I felt sorry for the princess, but not in order to gain an advantage for myself. To kill a husband and carry off a wife is something an honest man does not do. And since I am only an ordinary man, I prefer to die rather than do as you say."

Tsian Tang rose, apologized and said: "My words were over-hasty. I hope you will not take them ill!" And the King of the Dungting Sea also spoke kindly to him, and censured Tsian Tang because of his rude speech. So there was no more said about marriage.

On the following day Liu I took his leave, and the Queen of the Dungting Sea gave a farewell banquet in his honor.

With tears the queen said to Liu I: "My daughter owes you a great debt of gratitude, and we have not had an opportunity to make it up to you. Now you are going away and we see you go with heavy hearts!"

Then she ordered the princess to thank Liu I.

The princess stood there, blushing, bowed to him and said: "We will probably never see each other again!" Then tears choked her voice.

It is true that Liu I had resisted the stormy urging of her uncle, but when he saw the princess standing before him in all the charm of her loveliness, he felt sad at heart; yet he controlled himself and went his way. The

treasures which he took with him were incalculable.
The king and his brother themselves escorted him as
far as the river.

When, on his return home, he sold no more than a
hundredth part of what he had received, his fortune
already ran into the millions, and he was wealthier than
all his neighbors. He decided to take a wife, and heard
of a widow who lived in the North with her daughter.
Her father had become a Taoist in his later years and
had vanished in the clouds without ever returning. The
mother lived in poverty with the daughter; yet since
the girl was beautiful beyond measure she was seeking
a distinguished husband for her.

Liu I was content to take her, and the day of the wedding was set. And when he saw his bride unveiled on
the evening of her wedding day, she looked just like the
dragon-princess. He asked her about it, but she merely
smiled and said nothing.

After a time heaven sent them a son. Then she told
her husband: "To-day I will confess to you that I am
truly the Princess of Dungting Sea. When you had
rejected my uncle's proposal and gone away, I fell ill of
longing, and was near death. My parents wanted to
send for you, but they feared you might take exception
to my family. And so it was that I married you disguised
as a human maiden. I had not ventured to tell you until
now, but since heaven has sent us a son, I hope that
you will love his mother as well."

Then Liu I awoke as though from a deep sleep, and
from that time on both were very fond of each other.

One day his wife said: "If you wish to stay with me
eternally, then we cannot continue to dwell in the world
of men. We dragons live ten thousand years, and you
shall share our longevity. Come back with me to the Sea
of Dungting!"

Ten years passed and no one knew where Liu I, who had disappeared, might be. Then, by accident, a relative went sailing across the Sea of Dungting. Suddenly a blue mountain rose up out of the water.

The seamen cried in alarm: "There is no mountain on this spot! It must be a water-demon!"

While they were still pointing to it and talking, the mountain drew near the ship, and a gaily-colored boat slid from its summit into the water. A man sat in the middle, and fairies stood at either side of him. The man was Liu I. He beckoned to his cousin, and the latter drew up his garments and stepped into the boat with him. But when he had entered the boat it turned into a mountain. On the mountain stood a splendid castle, and in the castle stood Liu I, surrounded with radiance, and with the music of stringed instruments floating about him.

They greeted each other, and Liu I said to his cousin: "We have been parted no more than a moment, and your hair is already gray!"

His cousin answered: "You are a god and blessed: I have only a mortal body. Thus fate has decreed."

Then Liu I gave him fifty pills and said: "Each pill will extend your life for the space of a year. When you have lived the tale of these years, come to me and dwell no longer in the earthly world of dust, where there is nothing but toil and trouble."

Then he took him back across the sea and disappeared.

His cousin, however, retired from the world, and fifty years later, when he had taken all the pills, he disappeared and was never seen again.

The Maiden Who Was Stolen Away

IN THE WESTERN PORTION of the old capital city of Lo Yang there was a ruined cloister, in which stood an enormous pagoda, several hundred stories high. Three or four people could still find room to stand on its very top.

Not far from it there lived a beautiful maiden, and one very hot summer's day she was sitting in the courtyard of her home, trying to keep cool. And as she sat there a sudden cyclone came up and carried her off. When she opened her eyes, there she was on top of the pagoda, and beside her stood a young man in the dress of a student.

He was very polite and affable, and said to her: "It seems as though heaven had meant to bring us together, and if you promise to marry me, we will be very happy." But to this the maiden would not agree. So the student said that until she changed her mind she would have to remain on the pagoda-top. Then he produced bread and wine for her to satisfy her hunger and thirst, and disappeared.

Thereafter he appeared each day and asked her whether she had changed her mind, and each day she told him she had not. When he went away he always carefully closed the openings in the pagoda-top with stones, and he had also removed some of the steps of the stairs, so that she could not climb down. And when he came to the pagoda-top he always brought her food and drink, and he also presented her with rouge and powder, dresses and mandarin-coats and all sorts of jewelry. He told her he had bought them in the market-0place. And he also hung up a great carbuncle-stone, so that the pagoda-top was bright by night as well as by day. The maiden had all that heart could wish, and yet she was not happy.

But one day when he went away he forgot to lock the window. The maiden spied on him without his knowing it, and saw that from a youth he turned himself into an ogre, with hair as red as cherries and a face as black as coal. His eyeballs bulged out of their sockets, and his mouth looked like a dish full of blood. Crooked white fangs thrust themselves from his lips, and two wings grew from his shoulders. Spreading them, he flew down to earth and at once turned into a man again.

The maiden was seized with terror, and burst into tears. Looking down from her pagoda she saw a wanderer passing below. She called out, but the pagoda was so high that her voice did not carry down to him. She beckoned with her hand, but the wanderer did not look up. Then she could think of nothing else to do but to throw down the old clothes she had formerly worn. They fluttered through the air to the ground.

The wanderer picked up the clothes. Then he looked up at the pagoda, and quite up at the very top he saw a tiny figure which looked like that of a girl; yet he could not make out her features. For a long time he wondered who it might be, but in vain. Then he had an idea.

"My neighbor's daughter," said he to himself, "was carried away by a magic storm. Is it possible that she may be up there?"

So he took the clothes with him and showed them to the maiden's parents, and when they saw them they burst into tears.

But the maiden had a brother, who was stronger and braver than anyone for miles around. When the tale had been told him he took a heavy ax and went to the pagoda. There he hid himself in the tall grass and waited for what would happen. When the sun was just going down, along came a youth, tramping the hill. Suddenly he turned into an ogre, spread his wings and was about to fly. But the brother flung his ax at him and struck him on the arm. He began to roar loudly, and then fled to the western hills. But when the brother saw that it was impossible to climb the pagoda, he went back and enlisted the aid of several neighbors. With them he returned the following morning and they climbed up into the pagoda. Most of the steps of the stairway were in good condition, for the ogre had only destroyed those at the top. But they were able to get up with a ladder, and then the brother fetched down his sister and brought her safely home again.

And that was the end of the enchantment.

The Frog Princess

THERE WHERE THE Yangtze-kiang has come about halfway on its course to the sea, the Frog King is worshiped with great devotion. He has a temple there and frogs by the thousand are to be found in the neighborhood, some of them of enormous size. Those who incur the wrath of the god are apt to have strange visitations in their homes. Frogs hop about on tables and beds, and in extreme cases they even creep up the smooth walls of the room without falling. There are various kinds of omens, but all indicate that some misfortune threatens the house in question. Then the people living in it become terrified, slaughter a cow and offer it as a sacrifice. Thus the god is mollified and nothing further happens.

In that part of the country there once lived a youth named Sia-Kung-Schong. He was handsome and intelligent. When he was some six or seven years of age, a serving-maid dressed in green entered his home. She said that she was a messenger from the Frog King, and declared that the Frog King wished to have his daughter marry young Sia. Old Sia was an honest man, not very bright, and since this did not suit him, he declined the offer on the plea that his son was still too young to marry. In spite of this, however, he did not dare look about for another mate for him.

Then a few years passed and the boy gradually grew

68

up. A marriage between him and a certain Mistress Giang was decided upon.

But the Frog King sent word to Mistress Giang: "Young Sia is my son-in-law. How dare you undertake to lay claim to what does not belong to you!" Then Father Giang was frightened, and took back his promise.

This made Old Sia very sad. He prepared a sacrifice and went to his temple to pray. He explained that he felt unworthy of becoming the relation of a god. When he had finished praying a multitude of enormous maggots made their appearance in the sacrificial meat and wine, and crawled around. He poured them out, begged forgiveness, and returned home filled with evil forebodings. He did not know what more he could do, and had to let things take their course.

One day young Sia went out into the street. A messenger stepped up to him and told him, on the part of the Frog King, that the latter urgently requested Sia to come to him. There was no help for it; he had to follow the messenger. He led him through a red gateway into some magnificent, high-ceilinged rooms. In the great hall sat an ancient man who might have been some eighty years of age. Sia cast himself down on the ground before him in homage. The old man bade him rise, and assigned him a place at the table. Soon a number of girls and women came crowding in to look at him. Then the old man turned to them and said: "Go to the room of the bride and tell her that the bride-groom has arrived!"

Quickly a couple of maids ran away, and shortly after an old woman came from the inner apartments, leading a maiden by the hand, who might have been sixteen years of age, and was incomparably beautiful. The old man pointed to her and said: "This is my tenth little daughter. It seemed to me that you would make a good

pair. But your father has scorned us because of our dif-
ference in race. Yet one's marriage is a matter that is of
life-long importance. Our parents can determine it only
in part. In the end it rests mainly with oneself."

Sia looked steadily at the girl, and a fondness for her
grew in his heart. He sat there in silence. The old man
continued: "I knew very well that the young gentleman
would agree. Go on ahead of us, and we will bring you
your bride!"

Sia said he would, and hurried to inform his father.
His father did not know what to do in his excitement.
He suggested an excuse and wanted to send Sia back
to decline his bride with thanks. But this Sia was not
willing to do. While they were arguing the matter,
the bride's carriage was already at the door. It was surrounded by a crowd of greencoats, and the lady
entered the house, and bowed politely to her parents-
in-law. When the latter saw her they were both pleased,
and the wedding was announced for that very evening.

The new couple lived in peace and good understand-
ing. And after they had been married their divine
parents-in-law often came to their house. When they appeared dressed in red, it meant that some good fortune
was to befall them; when they came dressed in white, it
signified that they were sure to make some gain. Thus,
in the course of time, the family became wealthy.

But since they had become related to the gods the
rooms, courtyards and all other places were always
crowded with frogs. And no one ventured to harm
them. Sia Kung-Schong alone was young and showed no
consideration. When he was in good spirits he did not
bother them, but when he got out of sorts he knew no
mercy, and purposely stepped on them and killed them.

In general his young wife was modest and obedient;
yet she easily lost her temper. She could not approve
her husband's conduct. But Sia would not do her the

*The rooms, courtyards, and all other places
were always crowded with frogs.*

favor to give up his brutal habit. So she scolded him because of it and he grew angry.

"Do you imagine," he told her, "that because your parents can visit human beings with misfortune, that a real man would be afraid of a frog?"

His wife carefully avoided uttering the word "frog," hence his speech angered her, and she said: "Since I have dwelt in your house your fields have yielded larger crops, and you have obtained the highest selling-prices. And that is something, after all. But now, when young and old, you are comfortably established, you wish to act like the fledgling owl, who picks out his own mother's eyes as soon as he is able to fly!"

Sia then grew still more angry, and answered: "These gifts have been unwelcome to me for a long time, for I consider them unclean. I could never consent to leave such property to sons and grandsons. It would be better if we parted at once!"

So he bade his wife leave the house, and before his parents knew anything about it, she was gone. His parents scolded him and told him to go at once and bring her back. But he was filled with rage, and would not give in to them.

That same night he and his mother fell sick. They felt weak and could not eat. The father, much worried, went to the temple to beg for pardon. And he prayed so earnestly that his wife and son recovered in three days' time. And the Frog Princess also returned, and they lived together happily and contented as before.

But the young woman sat in the house all day long, occupied solely with her ornaments and her rouge, and did not concern herself with sewing and stitching. So Sia Kung-Schong's mother still had to look out for her son's clothes.

One day his mother was angry and said: "My son has a wife, and yet I have to do all the work! In other homes the daughter-in-law serves her mother-in-law. But in our house the mother-in-law must serve the daughter-in-law."

This the princess accidentally heard. In she came, much excited, and began: "Have I ever omitted, as is right and proper, to visit you morning and evening? My only fault is that I will not burden myself with all this toil for the sake of saving a trifling sum of money!" The mother answered not a word, but wept bitterly and in silence because of the insult offered her.

Her son came along and noticed that his mother had been weeping. He insisted on knowing the reason, and found out what had happened. Angrily he reproached his wife. She raised objections and did not wish to admit that she had been in the wrong. Finally Sia said: "It is better to have no wife at all than one who gives her mother-in-law no pleasure. What can the old frog do to me after all, if I anger him, save call misfortunes upon me and take my life!" So he once more drove his wife out of the house.

The princess left her home and went away. The following day fire broke out in the house, and spread to several other buildings. Tables, beds, everything was burned.

Sia, in a rage because of the fire, went to the temple to complain: "To bring up a daughter in such a way that she does not please her parents-in-law shows that there is no discipline in a house. And now you even encourage her in her faults. It is said the gods are most just. Are there gods who teach men to fear their wives? Incidentally, the whole quarrel rests on me alone. My parents had nothing to do with it. If I was to be punished by the ax and cord, well and good. You could have carried out the punishment yourself. But this you did not do. So now I will burn your own house in order to satisfy my own sense of justice!"

With these words he began piling up brushwood before the temple, struck sparks and wanted to set it ablaze. The neighbors came streaming up, and pleaded with him. So he swallowed his rage and went home.

When his parents heard of it, they grew pale with a great fear. But at night the god appeared to the people of a neighboring village, and ordered them to rebuild the house of his son-in-law. When day began to dawn they dragged up building-wood, and the workmen all came in throngs to build for Sia. No matter what he said he could not prevent them. All day long hundreds of workmen were busy. And in the course of a few days all the rooms had been rebuilt, and all the utensils, curtains and furniture were there as before. And when the work had been completed the princess also returned. She climbed the stairs to the great room, and acknowledged her fault with many tender and loving words. Then she turned to Sia-Kung-Schong, and smiled at him sideways. Instead of resentment, joy now filled the whole house. And after that time the princess was especially peaceable. Two whole years passed without an angry word being said.

But the princess had a great dislike for snakes. Once, by way of a joke, young Sia put a small snake into a parcel, which he gave her and told her to open. She turned pale and reproached him. Then Sia-Kung-Schong also took his jest seriously, and angry words passed.

At last the princess said: "This time I will not wait for you to turn me out. Now we are finally done with one another!" And with that she walked out of the door.

Father Sia grew very much alarmed, beat his son himself with his staff, and begged the god to be kind and forgive. Fortunately there were no evil consequences. All was quiet and not a sound was heard.

Thus more than a year passed. Sia-Kung-Schong longed for the princess and took himself seriously to task. He would creep in secret to the temple of the god, and lament because he had lost the princess. But no voice answered him. And soon afterward he even heard that the god had betrothed his daughter to another man. Then he grew hopeless at heart, and thought of finding another wife for himself. Yet no matter how he searched he could find none who equalled the princess. This only increased his longing for her, and he went to the home of the Yuans, to a member of which family it was said she had been promised. There they had already painted the walls, and swept the courtyard, and all was in readiness to receive the bridal carriage. Sia was overcome with remorse and discontent. He no longer ate, and fell ill. His parents were quite stunned by the anxiety they felt on his account, and were incapable of helpful thought.

He opened his eyes and it was the princess.

Suddenly, while he was lying there only half-conscious, he felt someone stroke him, and heard a voice say: "And how goes it with our real husband, who insisted on turning out his wife?"

He opened his eyes and it was the princess.

Full of joy he leaped up and said: "How is it you have come back to me?" The princess answered: "To tell the truth, according to your own habit of treating people badly, I should have followed my father's advice and taken another husband. And, as a matter of fact, the wedding gifts of the Yuan family have been lying in my home for a long time. But I thought and thought and could not bring myself to do so. The wedding was to have been this evening, and my father thought it shameful to have the wedding gifts carried back. So I took the things myself and placed them before the

Yuans' door. When I went out my father ran out beside me: 'You insane girl,' he said, 'so you will not listen to what I say! If you are ill-treated by Sia in the future I wash my hands of it. Even if they kill you, you shall not come home to me again!'"

Moved by her faithfulness, the tears rolled from Sia's eyes. The servants, full of joy, hurried to the parents to acquaint them with the good news. And when they heard it they did not wait for the young people to come to them, but hastened themselves to their son's rooms, took the princess by the hand and wept. Young Sia, too, had become more settled by this time, and was no longer so mischievous. So he and his wife grew to love each other more sincerely day by day.

Once the princess said to him: "Formerly, when you always treated me badly, I feared that we would not keep company into our old age. So I never asked heaven to send us a child. But now all that has changed, and I will beg the gods for a son."

And, sure enough, before long Sia's parents-in-law appeared in the house clad in red garments, and shortly after heaven sent the happy pair two sons instead of one.

From that time on their intercourse with the Frog-King was never interrupted. When someone among the people had angered the god, he first tried to induce young Sia to speak for him, and sent his wife and daughter to the Frog Princess to implore her aid. And if the princess laughed, then all would be well.

The Sia family has many descendants, whom the people call "the little frog men." Those who are near them do not venture to call them by this name, but those standing further off do so.